KIDS HAVE FEELINGS, TOO

Moving Is Hard

By Joan Singleton Prestine
Illustrations by Virginia Kylberg

McGraw-Hill
Children's Publishing

McGraw-Hill
Children's Publishing

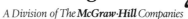

A Division of The McGraw·Hill Companies

©2003 McGraw-Hill Children's Publishing

Send all inquiries to:
McGraw-Hill Children's Publishing
8787 Orion Place
Columbus, OH 43240-4027

ISBN 1-57768-681-0

Library of Congress Cataloging-in-Publication Data is on file with the publisher.

Printed in the United States of America.

1 2 3 4 5 6 7 8 9 PHXBK 01 02 03 04 05 06 07 08 09

We've lived here for a long time. In this house. In this neighborhood. I like it here.

I play baseball with my neighborhood friends.

Scott and Debbie and Jeff and I trade books at the bus stop.

Buckles and I run in the fields.

I climb tall trees and spy on my whole world.

But now we are moving. I don't want to move. All my friends live here. I like this house and this neighborhood and I especially like my room.

Moving is hard. Our new house isn't a house. It's an apartment. And this neighborhood isn't a neighborhood. It's busy streets and tall buildings. There's no place to play baseball. I'll never use my mitt again.

I don't ride the school bus. There is no school bus. And I don't have any friends. I'll never trade books again.

There aren't any fields where Buckles and I can run. We'll never run together again.

There aren't any tall trees. There are only little baby trees. I'll never spy on my whole world again. Even though I didn't want to, we moved anyway.

Then I found out there's a baseball league. Now I play first base.

I carpool to school with Tonya and José.
We're friends and we trade books in the car.

I even found a park. Buckles and I can run and run.

27

The best thing I found was a secret stairway that leads to the roof of my apartment building. I can spy on my whole world.

And my new room
is even better than my old one.

E ven though I didn't want to move, we had to. I haven't lived here long. But I've decided that this apartment is a lot like my old house—only different. And these streets and buildings are a lot like my old neighborhood—only different. Even though moving is hard, I like it here. In my new apartment house. In my new neighborhood.

RED HOT HOT DOGS

Discussing **Moving Is Hard** With Children

After reading the story, encourage discussion. Children learn from sharing their thoughts and feelings.

Discussion Questions for **Moving Is Hard**

- How did the girl feel about her new home when she first moved in? What did she miss? What was different?
- What did the girl do first when she moved into her new home? What would be the first thing you would do?
- How did her feelings change after she'd lived there for a while? What made them change?
- At the end of the story, what did she like about her new home?

Significance of **Moving Is Hard** for Children

Sometimes a book will trigger strong feelings in young children, especially if they have experienced similar situations. If they feel comfortable, encourage children to share their experiences. **Helping Children Cope With Moving** is a resource guide for **Moving Is Hard**. The guide is for adults to use with children. It includes suggestions for talking about moving, describes how children respond to their feelings, and offers several hands-on projects that may help children adjust to their new environments.